Mister Penny's Race Horse

Also Written and Illustrated by Marie Hall Ets

Play with Me

Another Day

Beasts and Nonsense

Mr. T. W. Anthony Woo

Little Old Automobile

Oley: The Sea Monster

In the Forest

Mister Penny

The Story of a Baby

By Ellen Tarry and Marie Hall Ets

My Dog Rinty

Mister Penny's Race Horse

BY MARIE HALL ETS

Limpy

Mister Penny

NEW YORK · THE VIKING PRESS · 1956

To A.E., with thanks for taking me to so many fairs

ALL summer Mister Penny and his family worked in their garden. By fall their vegetables and flowers were so big and beautiful that Mister Penny decided to show them at the fair.

And I'll show my animals too, he said to himself. All but Limpy.

5

Limpy is too old and knobby. The judges would only laugh at him, though to me he's the most beautiful horse in the world—and the wisest one too.

So before the fair started, Mister Penny went to the village of Wuddle and got the tags that he needed. He got tags for his vegetables and flowers. Then he got tags for his animals. He got

6

one for Mooloo his cow, one for Splop his goat, one for Pugwug his pig, one for Mimkin his lamb, one for Chukluk his hen, one for Doody his rooster—but none for Limpy. And then, because he had no wagon in which to carry his things to the fair, he stopped at the Widow Smile's and borrowed an old two-wheeled cart that she didn't use any more.

7

"You mustn't feel bad because you are not going to be in the fair," he said to Limpy when he came home with the tags and the cart. "You know about judges. They won't look at old fellows like us. But remember this, Limpy. Without you we wouldn't have any garden at all. And without you to pull the cart we couldn't get our things to the fair grounds."

Now Limpy had never had anything to pull but a plow, so he was happy to have the cart. But still, he was sad that he wasn't going to be in the fair like the others. He thought that the bandage on his lame leg made him look like a race horse, and he wanted people to see him. *And* he wanted to run on the race track.

"And if we win enough prizes so we have the money," Mister Penny told him, "you can all have a ride on the Ferris wheel."

The thought of a ride way up into the air on the Ferris wheel made Mister Penny's family so happy that they could scarcely wait for the fair to start. Whenever Splop, the goat, thought about it she kicked her feet in all directions and butted. She butted at anything or anyone around.

"Don't be so sure we are going to get that ride," said Limpy one day when Splop was kicking and butting. "It takes a lot of money to buy rides for a family like ours. Mister Penny will have to win a lot of prizes."

"Don't worry!" said Splop. "We'll win enough prizes! Haven't

we got the biggest pumpkin in the world? And the biggest sunflowers? And doesn't Mooloo give more milk than any other cow in the world?"

"Maybe so," said Limpy. "But we can't be sure until the judges have given out the prizes."

"I'm not going to wait for the judges!" said Splop. "I'm going to find out as soon as we get to the fair grounds."

"How?" asked Mooloo.

"I'll just go and see for myself," said Splop. "For instance, I'll come in your tent, and if no other cow has a milk bag as big as yours I'll *know* that you're going to get first prize."

"Don't be foolish!" said Limpy. "You can't leave your own tent. You'd just be caught and make trouble for Mister Penny."

"Not if I go in the night," said Splop.

"That shows how much you don't know about fairs," said Limpy. "The owners sleep right there in the tent with the cows and watch them."

"Well, no one sleeps with the vegetables and flowers, do they?" asked Splop. "And any goat worth her name can get out in the night and into those tents without getting caught."

"And any rooster worth *his* name can get into any place he

wants in the night without getting caught," said Doody. "I'll go with you, Splop. I want to know too if we're going to get that ride on the Ferris wheel."

But just then Mister Penny came out to say thank you and good night to the sun—as he did every day—so the animals had to stop talking. For animals never want people to know that they talk to one another when they are alone.

The fair was to start on Wednesday. On Tuesday, Mister Penny was up before light, getting ready, for he had to have all his things at the fair grounds by two in the afternoon. He put blankets and hay and bags of feed in the cart, so his animals would have something to sleep on and plenty to eat, and two sheets for himself.

Then he put in the big pumpkin—it was so big that his arms only reached halfway around it—and his prettiest cabbages, and four ears of corn on a red plate, and six of Chukluk's biggest eggs in a basket. I'll cut the flowers last, he said to himself. I don't want them to fade. And he started washing his animals.

He washed Mimkin first. Then he polished her toes and clipped the wool on her back to make it smooth and flat, but he left curls on her forehead. Then he took her out to the cart. Next he washed Chukluk and Doody and oiled their feathers and polished their beaks and nails. Then it was Pugwug's turn, and Mister Penny used a scrub brush on him. The poor pig squirmed and squealed and tried to get away—not because the brush hurt, but because he didn't like to be washed with water. He'd rather have mud baths. But at last he was all pink and clean, with shining toes and an extra curl in his tail.

"As sweet and pretty a little pig as ever I did see!" said Mister Penny as he carried him out to the cart.

Then Mister Penny went back for Mooloo and Splop. "There's
no use washing you two now," he told them, "because you have to
walk and you'll only get dirty again. I'll wash you at the fair

tomorrow." And he led them out and tied them to the back of the cart. Then he went for the flowers.

He cut the three giant sunflowers and put them in a milk can of water. Then he cut a bunch of beautiful pink roses and put them in a big pail. Then he harnessed Limpy and hitched him to the cart. "You don't have to be washed and fixed up," he told Limpy, "because no one's going to be looking at you."

16

And now that everything else was ready Mister Penny went in for his coat and hat and came back and picked up the reins. "All right, Limpy," he said. "Let's go."

But Limpy wouldn't move. If he was going to pull a load like other horses, he wanted *his* driver to ride too, like theirs.

"Come on!" said Mister Penny. "If I get on too the load will be too heavy. Giddap! Let's go!" But still Limpy wouldn't move.

So at last Mister Penny climbed on, and they started off.

At the top of the first hill past Wuddle, Doody, who was riding on Limpy's back, stood up and started crowing. "I see it! I do, oo-OO, oo-OOOOOOOOOOOOO!" he crowed.

The other animals lifted their heads—all but Pugwug, who was sleeping—and they saw it too. *A great big Ferris wheel!* Splop

kicked her feet and butted. Mooloo said, "Moooo! Me tooooo!" and
went on chewing her cud as fast as she could so that she would have
more milk than any other cow at the fair.

"I know how much you all want to ride on the Ferris wheel,"
said Mister Penny. "I hope we win enough prizes so you can."

Over the next hill they came to the gate of the fair grounds,

and went in without stopping, for the fair hadn't opened yet and no one had to pay. Then they started driving around the grounds, leaving everything where it belonged. They stopped first at the main building just inside the gate, and Mister Penny carried the three giant sunflowers and the roses in there. Next they stopped at a tent marked CATTLE, and Mister Penny took Mooloo in there

and tied her to the fence at one side. And he left a blanket and some straw and hay and a big bag of feed too. Then they came to the **HOME GARDENERS'** tent, and Mister Penny carried the big pumpkin and the three cabbages and the plate of corn and the basket of eggs in there. Next they came to the **POULTRY** tent.

"And this is where you go," Mister Penny said to Chukluk and

Doody, and carried them in and put them in two of the empty cages. "I know you won't like it here," he said as he fastened the cages. "But it's just for three days. And I'll be back to take care of you."

The last tent in the row was marked SHEEP AND SWINE. At one end were pens for young pigs, and at the other end were pens for lambs, and in the middle were a few pens for goats. Mister Penny carried Pugwug and Mimkin in and put them in the pens where they belonged.

Then he led Splop in and put her in a pen in the middle. "I'm not going to tie you," he told her, "because you don't like it and always get tangled in the rope. But try not to be too rambunctious. This board at the side is so wobbly it will fall if you bump it."

Splop looked at the board and smiled. That was just what she wanted. But she must wait until dark.

And now, since everything had been delivered, Mister Penny

drove Limpy back through the fair grounds and on out to the big field inside the race track where the farmers parked their horses and wagons. There was a vacant space by the fence near the judges' stand, so Mister Penny drove in there. He unharnessed Limpy and tied him to the back of the cart with a rope long enough so that the horse could reach the grass all around, and put some hay and oats

in the back of the cart for him too. And then, because the flies were biting, Mister Penny covered Limpy with one of the sheets he had brought for his own bed, and fastened it on with safety pins. "Just like a race horse," he said patting Limpy's back. Then he took some pails and pans for water, and a bag of feed, and went back to the tents to take care of his animals there.

Now Limpy had a chance to look around. All the other horses in the field had wagons or buggies with four wheels. He was just wishing his cart had four wheels when he noticed the race horses on the other side of the fence, whose drivers were running them up and down the track for practice. Well, switch my tail! he said to himself. The race carts have only two wheels. My cart is a race cart

and I didn't know it! I'd rather be a race horse than a farm horse, any day! And he began wishing he could go out and run on the race track. But no, he said to himself. I don't want to make trouble for Mister Penny and lose those rides on the Ferris wheel. So he started munching the grass at his feet, but his eyes were on the race horses on the other side of the fence.

27

That night after Mister Penny had gone from one animal to the other, giving them feed and water and making them comfortable, he made a bed for himself in the straw near Mooloo and was soon fast asleep.

But Splop, in the tent for SHEEP AND SWINE, was not asleep. She was wide awake and waiting. She waited until it was so dark no one could see her; then she butted down the board on the side of her pen. She couldn't go and look at the pigs and the lambs because some of the owners were sleeping near them. So she ducked under the side of the tent and went running down the road.

She stopped when she came to the tent where the chickens were and stuck her head through the flap. There were no people in there—she could tell by the gentle clucking and rustling the chickens in the cages were making. So she went in and started looking around.

When she had looked at all the hens she started kicking out her feet and butting, for Chukluk was the biggest one there. "That's one prize, anyway," said Splop, and went on to look at the roosters.

"And here's another prize!" crowed Doody. "No rooster here is as smart-looking as me! Let me out, Splop, so I can go with you to look in the other tents."

28

Splop stood on her hind legs and tried to pull out the wire that fastened the cage. She held it in her teeth and twisted and pulled. Then she grew impatient and gave such a yank that the door came open with a jerk, and back she fell against the cages behind her. Down they came. And down came Doody's cage too.

"Look-look-look-look-look-look OUT!" warned Chukluk, as all the chickens in the dumped-over cages started squawking and cackling like birds in a zoo. "Look-look-look-look-look OUT!"

But Splop and Doody didn't have to be warned. They were out of the tent and off down the road before anyone could come and catch them.

When they came to the main building near the gate they found everything closed but one little window up over the door. So Splop had to wait outside while Doody flew up and went in alone.

For a while all was quiet inside. Then Splop saw a light and heard yelling and crashing. The next minute Doody came flying out through the window again. "Run!" he was squawking. "Run!" And they both ran so fast that they were way down the road, hiding in a clump of tall weeds, before the door opened and a watchman came out with a lantern.

"What happened?" asked Splop, when the man had gone in again and shut the door. "And how about our flowers?"

"Our sunflowers were the biggest of all," said Doody. "But they all spilled on the floor when that man tried to catch me."

"Oh, Doody!" said Splop.

"I couldn't help it!" said Doody.

"Well, maybe our roses will win a prize, anyway," said Splop.
"Come on. Let's go look at the vegetables."

So they came out of the weeds and started on again, without
noticing that the weeds had stuck burrs all over them.

There was no one in the tent with the vegetables, so Splop and Doody ran from table to table, looking at all the things. At first they were very sad, for their eggs were not the biggest, and their corn was not the best, and their cabbages were not the prettiest. But when they came to the pumpkins and saw that their pumpkin was twice as big as any of the others, they were so excited they couldn't keep still. Doody flapped his wings and started crowing. And Splop started kicking and butting. But she wasn't watching what she butted and butted the end of the table. Down came the table. And down came all the pumpkins.

The other pumpkins rolled down without damage, but Mister Penny's pumpkin was so big and heavy that when it hit the ground it broke all to pieces.

For a while Splop and Doody just stood there and looked. But there was nothing they could do.

"Come on," said Splop. "Let's get out."

So they went out and started back to their own tents. But Splop was so sad about the pumpkin that she forgot to go in with Doody and fasten his cage again. And she forgot to put back the board on the side of her own pen. She just fell down in her straw

and started thinking about the Ferris wheel. Maybe now they'd never have a ride! Why hadn't she and Doody stayed where they belonged!

Early the next morning Mister Penny took Mooloo out to the washing rack and washed her with a hose and polished her toes. Then he cleaned her bed and put her back inside to wait for the judges. "Good Mooloo," he said, patting her side. "You have more milk than any other cow in the tent!" And he was so happy that he started humming to himself as he took his pail and brush and went on to wash Splop.

But when he got to the SHEEP AND SWINE tent he stopped humming. Two policemen were there, looking at Splop and her pen.

"Are you the owner of this goat?" asked one policeman. "Are you Mister Penny?"

"Yes, this is me," said Mister Penny.

"Well, we hate to tell you, old man," said the policeman, "but some goat got out in the night and raised Cain with the exhibits. There were a rooster and a goat. We found their tracks everywhere. The watchman in the main building almost caught the rooster, but it got away. This goat of yours is the only one not tied, and her board is down too."

Mister Penny looked at Splop. Splop was hiding her face in the straw. And those burrs on her back, he thought. She didn't get those here in her pen!

"Come along to the POULTRY tent," said the policemen. "When we picked up the cages, your rooster's was the only one not fastened."

Mister Penny couldn't speak. He just followed the policemen

in and out among the people on the roadway, back into the tent where the chickens were. Doody's cage had been fastened again, but Mister Penny saw that Doody, like Splop, was covered with burrs.

"It was my goat and my rooster," Mister Penny said to the

36

policemen. "I can tell by those burrs. But what can I do to make right the damage they've done?"

"Well, nobody's things were damaged but your own," said the policemen. "But we must ask you to take all your animals out of the fair before they can do more mischief."

Back in the field inside the race track, Limpy had stopped eating and was watching the race horses. *All* the race horses had been harnessed now and were running up and down the track, getting ready for the race. Limpy was so interested in watching that he didn't see Mister Penny coming back with Splop and Doody and Chukluk until Mister Penny spoke.

"I'm sorry, Limpy," Mister Penny said. "We've been ordered

38

out. We all have to go home again—without any prizes and without any ride on the Ferris wheel. I shouldn't have promised a ride on the Ferris wheel until we were sure of the prizes. Splop was too impatient, that's all."

Mister Penny put the chickens in the cart, tied Splop on behind, and turned the cart around. Then he took the sheet off Limpy, put on his harness, and hitched him to the cart. Without

39

bothering to tie Limpy, Mister Penny hurried off to get the other
animals.

"What happened?" Limpy asked Splop when Mister Penny
had gone. "What did you do to make trouble and spoil the fair for
us all?"

"It was these burrs," said Splop, trying to pull them off her
legs and tail. "Big old tattletales! If it hadn't been for these burrs—
and Mister Penny—no one could have been sure it was us who got

40

into the tents! Why does Mister Penny have to be so honest?"

"Yes," said Doody, picking at his breast. "It was these burrs! Big old tattletales!"

"Oh, Splop!" said Limpy. "I warned you! I told you that you would only make trouble if you got out! Now we all have to go home without *any* prizes and without our ride on the Ferris wheel —and maybe without even seeing a horse race!"

Without answering, Splop worked herself loose from the rope,

climbed into the cart, and sat down up in front. Several men had climbed into the judges' stand near them. Crowds of people were filling the seats in the grandstand. Some of the race horses were racing one another and running way off down the track. A clown with a honking goose under his arm went stumbling and falling along in front of the grandstand, making the people laugh.

I could make them laugh too, thought Limpy, if I had the chance. "Do you see?" he asked Splop and the chickens. "Race carts have just two wheels, like mine. I'm harnessed to a race cart. I should be out there racing too."

"Why not?" said Splop, picking up the reins and stretching her legs to look like the driver of a race horse.

After a little the starter, up in the judges' stand, began calling the numbers of the horses as they passed and telling the people their names. Why don't they hurry! thought Limpy. Why don't they *hurry!* If they don't hurry I won't even see the race before I have to go home!

When all the horses had passed and had their names called,

their drivers drove them back behind the starting line, ready to start. But the drivers had a hard time keeping them there. The horses stood on their hind legs and pranced and pulled on their bits to be off.

At last the bell clanged.

"Here they come!" said Limpy. "Here they come!"

But before the horses had reached the judges' stand, the bell clanged again for them all to go back and start over. And in the commotion of turning around, two carts bumped together and their wheels came off. So then those two horses were taken away to be hitched to other carts and everybody had to wait.

"Oh, why do they have to take so long!" said Splop, who never liked waiting for anything. Soon the people in the grand-stand got restless too, and started stomping and yelling for the race to start again.

"If this is a race cart," Splop said to Limpy, "why don't we go out there and show them how fast you can run?"

I wish I could! thought Limpy. I wish I could.

"We're all being sent home anyway," said Splop. "Nothing we do now could make more trouble for Mister Penny."

"Come on!" called the people. "Come on! Let's have a race!"

"All right!" whinnied Limpy, who thought they were calling to him. "All right! I'm coming!" And, rearing up on his hind legs

like the race horses, he turned and went galloping back across the field to the end of the fence and out onto the track.

"Come on!" he whinnied as he reached the race horses at the starting line. "Come on! Let's race!"

But the drivers of the race horses held them back, so Limpy raced on alone. Doody had flown onto his back and was holding

tight to the harness and crowing. Chukluk was clinging to the feedbag and squawking. And Splop was shaking the reins and baa-ing.

When the people in the grandstand heard the noise and saw Limpy coming down the track they stood up and started cheering and clapping. And that made Limpy run all the faster.

Now, Mister Penny had just come back to the fence near the judges' stand with Mooloo and Mimkin and Pugwug. When he saw

50

Limpy running away down the race track he started running after

him. "Stop, Limpy!" he called. "Stop! Stop!" And in his hurry to get

over the fence he dropped Mimkin and
Pugwug, and they started running
too. This made the people laugh
harder and harder.

Then the starter in the
judges' stand clanged the bell.

That means to go back
and start over, thought
Limpy. And he slowed up
and turned around and
came back at a trot, as the
race horses had, lifting high
his lame leg so the people
could see the bandage. That
made even the judges cheer.

Mister Penny picked up his hat,
then caught Limpy and started leading him off
at the side. But as he passed the judges' stand the director of the
fair, who was up there, called down to him. "Wait a minute, old
man!" called the director. "Wait a minute!"

What now? thought Mister Penny as he waited for the director
to come down. What will they do to me now?

"Are you the owner of this horse?" asked the director.

"I'm sorry," said Mister Penny. "He's never run away before. It's my fault. I shouldn't have left him untied."

"Sorry, *my hat!*" said the director. "Your old horse has just put on the funniest show this fair has ever seen! If you'll let him go on again this afternoon, and twice tomorrow, and twice Friday, I'll give you twenty-five dollars."

"Twenty-five dollars!" said Mister Penny. "Just to let my horse run away on the race track!" But then he remembered the policemen. "But I can't," he said sadly. "I've been ordered to take all my animals out of the fair." And he told the director what had happened.

"Forget it!" said the director. "I'll take care of all that. I'll have a tent put up right here in the field for you and your animals, so they won't have to stay in the show tents. And here they can see the races."

Mister Penny looked at his animals. Limpy was so happy his ears wiggled. But Splop, who had jumped down from the cart, started butting Mister Penny from behind. "Yes, I know, Splop," said Mister Penny, and he turned back to the director. "But there's one other thing," he said.

"What's that, old man?" said the director. "Speak up."

"Well, you see," said Mister Penny. "My animals don't care much for money. What they want is a ride on the Ferris wheel. And I promised them that."

54

"A ride on the *Ferris wheel?*" said the director. "*Animals?*
Animals on— *By Jove,* old man, what an idea! *What an idea!* Every-
one around Wuddle would hear of it if your animals rode on the
Ferris wheel and would come to see them on the track. Of course

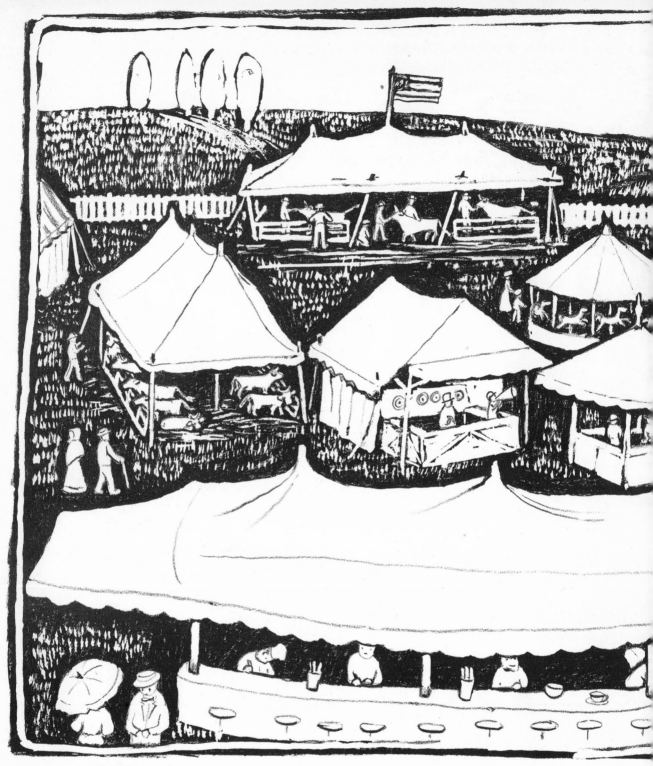

let them have their ride! I'll take them there myself—right now."

So Mister Penny left the cart in the field and he and his animals

went back through the fair with the director—who stopped and
bought them pink cotton candy on the way.

When they reached the Ferris wheel the director let them on without tickets, and the Ferris wheel carried them way up into the

air—so high it made them shiver to look down. (And Splop and Doody rode too, for Mister Penny said they could pay for their mischief after they got home.)

S WHEEL

TICKETS

That afternoon, and the next day, and the next, so many people came to see Limpy run on the race track that they couldn't all get seats in the grandstand. They had to stand behind the fences

and climb on the wagons in the field. And each time Limpy ran, then slowed up to show his bandage, such a cheer went up that it made his ears tingle, and he smiled and whinnied in reply.

The director said he had never seen anything like it. He was

so pleased that, when the fair was over, he gave Mister Penny fifty

dollars, instead of twenty-five, and made him promise to come back
next year with his race horse—and his other animals too.